Get **more** out of libraries

Please return or renew this item by the last date shown.
You can renew online at www.hants.gov.uk/library
Or by phoning 0845 603 5631

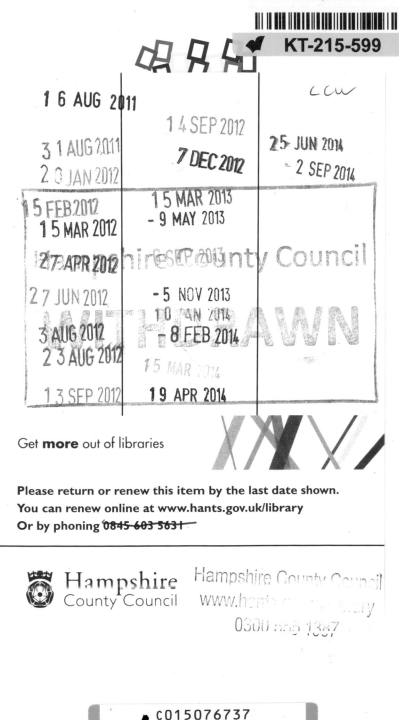

First published in 2008 by
Franklin Watts
338 Euston Road
London
NW1 3BH

Franklin Watts Australia
Level 17/207 Kent Street
Sydney
NSW 2000

Text © Anne Walter 2008
Illustration © Anni Axworthy 2008

A CIP catalogue record for this book is available
from the British Library.

ISBN 978 0 7496 7897 5 (hbk)
ISBN 978 0 7496 7903 3 (pbk)

Series Editor: Melanie Palmer
Series Advisor: Dr Barrie Wade
Series Designer: Peter Scoulding

Printed in China

Franklin Watts is a division of
Hachette Children's Books,
an Hachette Livre UK company.

HOPSCOTCH
FAIRY TALES

Goldilocks
and the
Three Bears

by Anne Walter and Anni Axworthy

W
FRANKLIN WATTS
LONDON•SYDNEY

Once upon a time, a little
girl called Goldilocks went
for a walk in the woods.

Three bears were also out in the woods. Their porridge was too hot, so they had decided to go for a walk while it cooled down.

Goldilocks found the bears' house in a part of the woods that she had never seen before.

By now, she was very hungry and she could smell something delicious coming from inside the house.

Goldilocks walked in and saw the three bowls of porridge. First, she tried the porridge in the biggest bowl. "Ouch! Too hot!" she cried.

11

Next, Goldilocks tried the porridge
in the medium-sized bowl.
"Yuck! Too cold!" she said.

Then she tried the porridge in the smallest bowl. "Just right!" she said, eating it all up.

After breakfast, Goldilocks wanted a rest. She sat in the biggest chair. "Ouch! Too hard!" she cried.

Next, she sat in the medium-sized chair. "Yuck! Too soft!" she cried.

Then she tried the smallest chair. "Just right!" she said. But as she was getting comfortable ...

CREAK

CRASH! The chair broke
into little pieces.

Goldilocks went upstairs and
found three beds. She lay down
on the biggest bed. "Ouch! Too
hard!" she said.

Next, Goldilocks tried the medium-sized bed. It was so soft that it nearly swallowed her up!

Then she tried the smallest bed.
It felt just right and she fell
fast asleep.

Meanwhile, the three bears were
finishing their walk.

"Shall we see if our porridge has
cooled down?" asked Mummy Bear.

"Yes," Baby Bear replied, "I'm hungry!" So the three bears hurried back for their breakfast.

"Who's been eating my porridge?"
roared Daddy Bear.
"Who's been eating my porridge?"
asked Mummy Bear.

"Who's been eating my porridge?"
cried Baby Bear. "They've eaten it
all up!"

"Who's been sitting in my chair?"
roared Daddy Bear.
"Who's been sitting in my chair?"
asked Mummy Bear.

"Who's been sitting in my chair? They've broken it!" cried Baby Bear.

"Who's been sleeping in my bed?"
roared Daddy Bear.
"Who's been sleeping in my bed?"
asked Mummy Bear.

"Look! Someone's still sleeping in my bed!" whispered Baby Bear.
"YES!" roared Daddy Bear, loudly.

Grrrrrrr!

Goldilocks woke up immediately. She jumped out of the window and ran home as fast as she could.

"What a rude little girl!' said
Daddy Bear.

Hopscotch has been specially designed to fit the requirements of the Literacy Framework. It offers real books by top authors and illustrators for children developing their reading skills. There are 55 Hopscotch stories to choose from:

Marvin, the Blue Pig
ISBN 978 0 7496 4619 6

Plip and Plop
ISBN 978 0 7496 4620 2

The Queen's Dragon
ISBN 978 0 7496 4618 9

Flora McQuack
ISBN 978 0 7496 4621 9

Willie the Whale
ISBN 978 0 7496 4623 3

Naughty Nancy
ISBN 978 0 7496 4622 6

Run!
ISBN 978 0 7496 4705 6

The Playground Snake
ISBN 978 0 7496 4706 3

"Sausages!"
ISBN 978 0 7496 4707 0

Bear in Town
ISBN 978 0 7496 5875 5

Pippin's Big Jump
ISBN 978 0 7496 4710 0

Whose Birthday Is It?
ISBN 978 0 7496 4709 4

The Princess and the Frog
ISBN 978 0 7496 5129 9

Flynn Flies High
ISBN 978 0 7496 5130 5

Clever Cat
ISBN 978 0 7496 5131 2

Moo!
ISBN 978 0 7496 5332 3

Izzie's Idea
ISBN 978 0 7496 5334 7

Roly-poly Rice Ball
ISBN 978 0 7496 5333 0

I Can't Stand It!
ISBN 978 0 7496 5765 9

Cockerel's Big Egg
ISBN 978 0 7496 5767 3

How to Teach a Dragon Manners
ISBN 978 0 7496 5873 1

The Truth about those Billy Goats
ISBN 978 0 7496 5766 6

Marlowe's Mum and the Tree House
ISBN 978 0 7496 5874 8

The Truth about Hansel and Gretel
ISBN 978 0 7496 4708 7

The Best Den Ever
ISBN 978 0 7496 5876 2

ADVENTURE STORIES

Aladdin and the Lamp
ISBN 978 0 7496 6692 7

Blackbeard the Pirate
ISBN 978 0 7496 6690 3

George and the Dragon
ISBN 978 0 7496 6691 0

Jack the Giant-Killer
ISBN 978 0 7496 6693 4

TALES OF KING ARTHUR

1. The Sword in the Stone
ISBN 978 0 7496 6694 1

2. Arthur the King
ISBN 978 0 7496 6695 8

3. The Round Table
ISBN 978 0 7496 6697 2

4. Sir Lancelot and the Ice Castle
ISBN 978 0 7496 6698 9

TALES OF ROBIN HOOD

Robin and the Knight
ISBN 978 0 7496 6699 6

Robin and the Monk
ISBN 978 0 7496 6700 9

Robin and the Silver Arrow
ISBN 978 0 7496 6703 0

Robin and the Friar
ISBN 978 0 7496 6702 3

FAIRY TALES

The Emperor's New Clothes
ISBN 978 0 7496 7421 2

Cinderella
ISBN 978 0 7496 7417 5

Snow White
ISBN 978 0 7496 7418 2

Jack and the Beanstalk
ISBN 978 0 7496 7422 9

The Three Billy Goats Gruff
ISBN 978 0 7496 7420 5

The Pied Piper of Hamelin
ISBN 978 0 7496 7419 9

Goldilocks and the Three Bears
ISBN 978 0 7496 7897 5 *
ISBN 978 0 7496 7903 3

Hansel and Gretel
ISBN 978 0 7496 7898 2 *
ISBN 978 0 7496 7904 0

The Three Little Pigs
ISBN 978 0 7496 7899 9 *
ISBN 978 0 7496 7905 7

Rapunzel
ISBN 978 0 7496 7900 2 *
ISBN 978 0 7496 7906 4

Little Red Riding Hood
ISBN 978 0 7496 7901 9 *
ISBN 978 0 7496 7907 1

Rumpelstiltskin
ISBN 978 0 7496 7902 6*
ISBN 978 0 7496 7908 8

HISTORIES

Toby and the Great Fire of London
ISBN 978 0 7496 7410 6

Pocahontas the Peacemaker
ISBN 978 0 7496 7411 3

Grandma's Seaside Bloomers
ISBN 978 0 7496 7412 0

Hoorah for Mary Seacole
ISBN 978 0 7496 7413 7

Remember the 5th of November
ISBN 978 0 7496 7414 4

Tutankhamun and the Golden Chariot
ISBN 978 0 7496 7415 1

* hardback